CLEVER MONKEY

Stephen Elboz

Illustrated by

Peter Bowman

OXFORD
UNIVERSITY PRESS

OXFORD
UNIVERSITY PRESS

Great Clarendon Street, Oxford, OX2 6DP,
United Kingdom

Oxford University Press is a department of the University of Oxford.
It furthers the University's objective of excellence in research, scholarship,
and education by publishing worldwide. Oxford is a registered trade mark of
Oxford University Press in the UK and in certain other countries

British Library Cataloguing in Publication Data
Data available

978-0-19-837735-1

5 7 9 10 8 6

Paper used in the production of this book is a natural, recyclable product
made from wood grown in sustainable forests. The manufacturing process
conforms to the environmental regulations of the country of origin.

Printed in China by Leo Paper Products Ltd.

Acknowledgements
Cover and inside illustrations by Peter Bowman
Inside cover notes written by Becca Heddle

This book is for Shaun Dunnett

Contents

Chapter 1

The Lost Keys

My name is Sandy Longtail. I live with my Mum and Dad and my sister Jem at Monkey Land Safari Park, home of the most intelligent monkeys in the whole world. It's a nice place to live. Trouble is, nothing much ever happens here …

Then one day, exciting news reached my tree.

The head keeper, Mr Otterbank, had lost his big bunch of keys. And a monkey had found them!

An urgent meeting was called about it.

The meeting was held that night at the tree of Milton Grizzlefur, the cleverest monkey in all of Monkey Land.

He doesn't look clever though. That's because he spends all day in a tyre hanging from an old tree.

(I say it looks like he's fast asleep.
"No, no," says Mum. "Not asleep. Milton
Grizzlefur is thinking.")

We all stood waiting for Milton
Grizzlefur to wake up – I mean, to stop
thinking.

At last he opened one yellow eye.

"Ah, yes, as I was saying," he said,
his grey whiskers looking a bit like a
human's beard.

"You weren't saying anything at all," I
thought. But I kept quiet about it.

"The keys," continued Milton Grizzlefur, "and what to do with them. Of course, we shall give them back. But the question is … Do we do it at once, or shall we – hmm – have a little fun with them first?"

His tyre spun him round the wrong way. This gave me and the other monkeys time to think.

We all knew what Milton Grizzlefur was getting at. It was the dearest wish of every monkey there to see the world outside Monkey Land.

We knew there was a lot to see. Nearly every night, Milton Grizzlefur read out the most interesting bits from a newspaper, rescued from the rubbish bin. But although we had learned many things about the world, it was not the same as seeing it with our own eyes.

By the time the tyre had turned Milton Grizzlefur back again, most monkeys had made up their mind.

Dad cleared his throat.

"Before we give Mr Otterbank his keys back, I would like to see what lies behind the big wire fence," he said. "For one night, I would like my freedom."

Monkey heads all around nodded in agreement. Oh look! Mine was nodding with them.

"But won't we need a disguise?" called Tonto Gribb, the big ginger monkey. "The humans will get nervous if they see a band of monkeys on the loose."

"That's true," added Mum. "It wouldn't be fair to get Mr Otterbank into trouble."

"Ah," said Milton Grizzlefur, "I've already thought of that. Anyone who wants to go on this little adventure, raise your paw."

Of course everyone did.

"Good, then follow me."

Chapter 2

Milton Grizzlefur's Plan

Milton Grizzlefur climbed down his tree. And because he was so old, he climbed slowly. He walked slowly too, stopping now and again to sniff the air.

"I wish he'd get a move on," said Jem. "Where do you think he's taking us?"

"How do I know, baboon face? It looks like Mr Otterbank's house."

And so it was.

We all stood at the wire gate leading into Mr Otterbank's garden.

The house was already dark. Mr Otterbank went to bed at sundown and got up again at sunrise.

Milton Grizzlefur said, "I have been looking at Mr Otterbank's keys. This one, for example, will open this gate, here."

Click. He had opened it. And before we knew it, we had followed him into Mr Otterbank's garden.

"This one will open Mr Otterbank's front door," Milton Grizzlefur went on, holding up a different key.

"How did Mr Otterbank manage to lock it, then?" asked Stanley Woolback, looking puzzled.

"Mrs Otterbank has a spare set of keys," Milton Grizzlefur explained.

Mum raised her paw to ask another question.

"Why do we need to get into Mr Otterbank's house at all?"

"Dear Mrs Longtail," said Milton Grizzlefur. "We need to borrow some human clothes. Only for the night, you understand. We need the clothes of Mr Otterbank, Mrs Otterbank and both their children."

("Wow," I thought. "I get to wear trousers!")

"Now," continued Milton Grizzlefur.
"I need a couple of volunteers, willing to
be our burglars, so to speak."

I was so excited, I jumped up in the
air. When I came down, I landed on
Dad's tail. Then he jumped in the air. He
jumped in surprise!

Milton Grizzlefur thought we were
volunteering.

"Well done, Otis and Sandy. In you
go!"

"But ... but ... "

Poor Dad. He was still 'but ...
butting' as we were pushed through Mr
Otterbank's door and into his hallway.

"Good luck," said Milton Grizzlefur.

Chapter 3

Hunt the Clothes

Dad and I wandered through a few
rooms, getting used to the dark.
Neither of us made a sound with our
paws.

"Dad," I whispered, "I've just had a
thought. Where do humans keep their
clothes?"

"How do I know?" said Dad. He was
still annoyed about his tail. "Fur has
always been good enough for me."

"What about in here?" I pulled open a likely-looking door.

A light came on. I jumped into the air and landed on a table.

Dad sighed and gently shut the door.

"That, Sandy, is called a fridge. Humans keep their food in it. I think we have to look upstairs."

We went along the hall and up the stairs. These are a good invention in houses, but they wouldn't work so well in trees.

"I can hear Mr Otterbank snoring," I giggled.

"Just as long as he doesn't hear *you*," said Dad, tweaking my ear. "Now, this is called a bedroom —"

We went inside. Mr and Mrs
Otterbank were two big lumps in a bed.
Some clothes were on a chair, and we
grabbed them.

"There must be more somewhere," said
Dad. "Look in those drawers. They pull
out, so be careful."

Soon we had a big pile of clothes
which we took out into the hallway.
Then Dad went to search in the children's
room. I opened a window and threw
out everything we had into the
garden.

Below me I heard the mutter of
monkey voices, saying things like:

"Has anyone got the other shoe?"

"Do purple and orange go together?"

And, "Paws off! I saw that first."

Dad came out with the children's
clothes, and he said it sounded like a real
old jumble sale. Before I could ask what
a jumble sale was, Dad tossed the clothes
out of the window. We hurried downstairs
and out of the house.

What a sight we saw.
Little humans!

That's what they looked like. Of
course, the clothes were rather large for
monkeys. (Even though Mr Otterbank
and his wife are quite small for humans.)
Everyone was busily turning up cuffs and
trousers.

I didn't recognize Mum and Jem. It
was a good job Mum called to us.

"Over here," she said. "I've saved you
some stuff."

When we were dressed, Milton
Grizzlefur inspected us. He was wearing
checked trousers and a cap. His ears still
stuck out a bit.

"You need to pull down your hats
to hide your faces," he said. "Scarves
will do just as well. I know it's hot.
You little monkeys, do up those buttons.
And for heaven's sake stop chewing them.
Good. Are we ready to face what lies
outside Monkey Land? Then off we go."

Chapter 4

Beyond the Fence

I don't mind telling you, I was more than a little bit scared as Milton Grizzlefur unlocked the main gateway and we all went under the sign that said: *WELCOME TO MONKEY LAND*. I even let Jem hold my paw.

We saw we were on the edge of a big town.

"Now," said Milton Grizzlefur, "we had better break up into little groups so the humans don't become suspicious. And

we'll go in different directions. Watch
out for traffic. Cars go much, much
faster outside Monkey Land. And above
all things, remember to behave like a
human. Always walk on your back two
legs. Now go. Everyone be back here an
hour before sunrise."

So we went our different ways in our
little monkey groups. Mum and Dad
gripped our paws for safety.

Milton Grizzlefur was right about the
traffic. It zoomed along faster than a
charging rhino.

There was so much to see. And so
much that Jem and I didn't understand,
and so much which had to be explained
to us.

Just then, Mum was telling us about something called a lettuce box.

She said, "I've heard that humans put lettuces in that slot and post them to hungry friends —" Then she suddenly stopped. "Oh, help! Look, Otis, humans!"

"Don't panic, dear," said Dad. "It'll be all right."

Some humans went by. They looked at us strangely.

"What an ugly bunch of people," said one, when they were several steps on.

"And they must be sweltering in those heavy clothes," said another.

They turned a corner and we all burst out laughing.

"That was close," said Dad. "Let's walk on the other side of the road. It's not so brightly lit."

As we were crossing the road, a dirty white van shot into view. Its horn blared. Its lights blazed.

"Look out!" screamed Mum.

We jumped for our lives. The van just missed us.

Dad went absolutely ape!

"You fool!" he yelled. "You could have killed us." And he jumped on a fence, beat his chest and shook his head from side to side, which monkeys only do if they are seriously angry.

Mum stayed calm. "For goodness sake, Otis! Remember what Milton said. Act human!"

But it was too late. The white van had screeched to a halt and was reversing back.

Chapter 5

Smeelly and Fogg

Dad should never have lost his temper
like that. He was sorry now. We all were.

Two humans got out of the van – one
was tall, the other was short. Yet even
the short one towered over us. We found
that frightening. Mum and Dad huddled
together with Jem and me in the middle.

The tall human was very smart. He
wore a flower in his buttonhole. (Later,
we found out his name was Bantam
Fogg.)

The short one smelt like – well, not very nice. He was called Chas Smeelly.

"Well, Chas," said Bantam Fogg.

"Well, Mr Fogg," said Chas Smeelly. His hand flew out and snatched off Dad's hat. "Just as we thought, Mr Fogg. Flaming gorillas!"

"Monkeys, Chas, monkeys," corrected Bantam Fogg. "From that Monkey Land place, no doubt. But these are no ordinary monkeys, Chas. Look at them. Pretending to be humans … I expect they can understand what we say, too. You'd best open the van doors, Chas."

Chas Smeelly grinned as he opened the doors. "Doors opened, Mr Fogg," he said.

"Good." And to us Bantam Fogg said, "Listen to me, you monkey chaps. You're coming with us. There's a little job I want you to do."

And we climbed inside the van, feeling very small and very frightened.

Chapter 6

A *Second* Burglary

The back of the van had no windows, so we couldn't see where we were going. It was very bumpy. Chas Smeelly drove fast and said a lot of bad words about other drivers.

Then the van slowed right down. It felt as if we were sneaking up to some place where we shouldn't be.

Then it stopped.

Chas Smeelly turned off the engine and Bantam Fogg looked back at us. His smile was as friendly as a shark's.

"Now listen, you monkey chaps,"
he said, smiling. "I want you two big
monkeys to do a job for us. Here's what I
want you to do. This is Hambone Hall, a
big house full of lovely expensive things. I
want you to climb up and get in through
the top window."

He went on. "Then I want you to
start collecting up some of those lovely
things. Collect as many as you can and
bring them back to me and Mr Smeelly.
We'll be waiting here, ready to fill our
sacks."

Chas Smeelly turned around and the smell of him seemed to get stronger. "And just so you don't try any monkey business, like escaping, we'll keep the two little monkeys in the van for ..." he grinned, "... safety."

Mum looked at Dad. For the second
time in one night there was going to be a
burglary. But this was proper burglary.
Chas Smeelly and Bantam Fogg were
going to keep everything for themselves.

Poor Mum and Dad. There was
nothing they could do about it.

The van doors opened, and they slowly
climbed out.

"We'll be back soon," said Mum. She
looked so worried.

Then they were gone.

"Oh, Sandy!" wailed Jem, jumping up and down.

"Quiet in there," hissed Chas Smeelly. "Or I'll make you two into a pair of furry mittens!"

We stood up on our back legs and looked over the front seats and through the windscreen. There was a big house and Bantam Fogg was pointing up at one of its dark windows.

We saw Dad and Mum take off their shoes. Then they began to climb up a drainpipe.

After that, I couldn't bear to look.
I turned away and when I did,
I saw something that made me
whoop with joy.

"Don't do that!" said Jem, angrily.

"But, Jem. Look —"

I pointed with my paw.

"It's a key," said Jem. "Haven't keys got us into enough trouble tonight?"

"But that's not a door key," I said. "It's a key to start up the engine. I know because I've watched humans in the car park. If we can drive this thing, we can go and get help."

"And you reckon you can drive it?" Jem asked, excitedly.

"Of course!" I said, even though I wasn't really that sure.

And the next moment I was sitting in the driving seat, clutching the steering wheel with my paws, all four of them!

Chapter 7

In the Driving Seat

It was then that I found out that vans
are not made for monkeys to drive.

I couldn't see out of the windscreen.
Jem would have to give me directions.
She would also have to stand on the
pedals to make the van go or stop. I
explained to Jem how the pedals
worked.

"Brake ... accelerator," she repeated.

It was crowded in the driving seat. Jem had to stand on tiptoe and put her head out of the side window to see.

"Ready?" I said.

"I suppose so," she said.

I turned the key.

The engine came alive. "Accelerator!" I shouted at Jem. Suddenly we were rushing forward. Outside, I could hear Bantam Fogg and Chas Smeelly snarling. Their running feet crunched on the gravel as they chased after us.

Bam! We hit a statue and knocked off its head.

"Which way, Jem?" I hollered.

"Left!" she cried.

Baff! A different statue lost both its arms.

"Sorry, I meant right."

We clipped a tree and the main gateposts before we were back on the road. Luckily, we had left Bantam Fogg and Chas Smeelly far behind.

After a mile or two, Jem and I became much better. A team, you might say. I began to feel proud of myself. But the van must have looked very odd – as if it were driving itself!

Certainly, that was what it looked like to PC Duffle. He was parked in a side street, eating a sandwich. He shook his head. "Nah. Must be a trick of the light," he told himself, as we drove by.

Following the signs, we came in sight of Monkey Land. Jem was so excited, she forgot to do one small, important thing: brake.

CRASH! We went right through the gates and ended up outside Mr Otterbank's house.

A light went on. A window flew open. And Mr Otterbank's head poked out.

"It's a van," he said, turning to Mrs Otterbank, who was in bed with the sheets pulled up to her chin.

"Well I never – Sandy and Jem have just climbed out. And … and Sandy is writing something with his paw in the dirt beside the van.

"Let me see … *HELP! Mum and Dad prisoners at Hambone Hall. Come quickly.* I'd better go and see what this is all about."

It was then that he discovered all of his clothes had gone.

"Every drawer and cupboard empty!" he wailed.

Luckily, Mrs Otterbank remembered there was something he could wear. Something Mr Otterbank had worn at a fancy dress party last New Year's Eve.

Chapter 8

Two Mean Monkeys and One Angry Gorilla

Jem and me both screamed when a big, hairy gorilla stepped out of Mr Otterbank's house.

"It's only me," said Mr Otterbank's muffled voice. "Quickly, back inside the van, both of you. No, *I'll* drive now, if you don't mind."

He reversed the van past the shattered gates and we were off again.

Meanwhile, PC Duffle had finished
his sandwich and was eating a chocolate
cake. "Hmm," he thought. "Isn't that the
white van that looked like it didn't have a
driver? I'll look more carefully this time."

And so he did.

"That's all right," he said with a sigh
of relief. "There's a gorilla at the wheel …
A GORILLA?"

A second later, a half-eaten chocolate cake was tossed aside. Blue lights flashed and a siren wailed.

I tugged at Mr Otterbank's sleeve. Mr Otterbank glanced in the mirror.

"No time to stop now, Sandy," he said, and he raced on until he reached Hambone Hall.

In the headlights, we saw Bantam
Fogg and Chas Smeelly. Mum and Dad
were filling open sacks with treasure from
the house.

They all looked surprised when the van
screeched to a halt and a gorilla sprang
out, with two mean-looking monkeys on
either side of him.

"Hold it right there!" cried Mr
Otterbank.

"Hold it yourself," shouted Bantam Fogg, throwing a sack of treasure at him.

A big fight started: gorilla and monkeys against burglars. And then PC Duffle arrived.

He climbed out of his patrol car looking very confused.

He decided to arrest the gorilla for speeding.

But when he got him in a headlock, Mr Otterbank's mask came off.

That was too much for PC Duffle. He was so shocked that he fainted.

Outnumbered now five to two, Bantam Fogg and Chas Smeelly were quickly defeated. Mum and Dad sat on them and Mr Otterbank ran to get some rope from the van to tie them up.

"Ever been made a monkey of?" said Mr Otterbank cheerily.

Chas Smeelly used some more of his bad words. He really did know quite a few.

With the help of Mum and Dad, Mr Otterbank put Bantam Fogg and Chas Smeelly into the patrol car, with a note which read: *Arrest these two villains. They use innocent monkeys as burglars.* Me and Jem put the treasure nearby for evidence.

Mr Otterbank said, "Now, let's get out of here before that policeman comes to his senses."

Nobody had to be told twice. We jumped into the van, and Mr Otterbank drove off.

He didn't say much as he drove. It seemed like he was busy thinking.

And when he saw lots of little figures in badly-fitting shoes and clothes hurrying back to Monkey Land, he slowed down and became even more thoughtful.

He stopped outside his house and turned to Dad. "Otis," he said, "I am going back to bed. Please make sure that all the things you borrowed are left on my doorstep. And the keys, too. Goodnight."

And he went inside.

"Well," said Mum, surprised. "I thought he'd be more angry than that."

Chapter 9

What Mr Otterbank Did Next

Next morning in Monkey Land was pretty much like any other, as far as the visitors were concerned. But for the monkeys there were a lot of stories to be swapped. And everyone wondered what Mr Otterbank would do.

Clifton Moke said he expected Mr Otterbank would build an electric fence.

Jem's friend, Crystal, said it was more likely he would dig a moat and fill it with crocodiles.

But I knew Mr Otterbank wasn't like that at all. I was right. About a week later, several big plastic bags of old clothes appeared by the tyre tree.

And on a twig was a newly cut set of keys and a note which said: *Use these wisely.*

Of course, a meeting had to be held about what this might mean. Everyone gathered at the tyre tree.

Milton Grizzlefur sat high up in his tyre, scratching himself and waiting for silence. At last he began to speak.

"Mr Otterbank is the best human who ever lived," he told us. "He realizes we are not ordinary monkeys. He knows we need to see the outside world from time to time … And it looks like he's given us permission to do so. But listen to me, monkeys. We have to be much more careful in future."

"You can say that again," I muttered.

Later I went for a nap in my favourite tree.

"You know," I thought to myself, as I was falling asleep, "the outside world's all right, but ... yawn ... really, there's no place like home."

About the author

I don't like zoos or animal parks. I always feel so sorry for the animals that I want to let them out ... Luckily, the monkeys in my story don't need me to do that for them. They are clever enough to get out all by themselves.

Although, now I come to think about it, the idea of meeting a monkey on a bus or in a supermarket might be rather alarming!